DON

and the

BOOK BUS

DON
and the
BOOK BUS

by

HELEN D. OLDS

drawings by

URSULA KOERING

NEW YORK : ALFRED·A·KNOPF

L. C. Catalog Card Number: 56–5081

© HELEN D. OLDS AND URSULA KOERING, 1956

THIS IS A BORZOI BOOK,
PUBLISHED BY ALFRED A. KNOPF, INC.

To

my twin brother

HOWARD F. DIEHL

who, on our tenth birthday,

gave me the best gift I ever received—

his library card!

DON

and the

BOOK BUS

"O. K., I'll go with you." Don Tracy couldn't see why his twin sister, Dorry, was so excited about the Book Bus. But he followed her out of their new home, which was a trailer.

They had never lived in a trailer city before, and had arrived only last night.

All about there were trailers—streets and streets of them, nearly a thousand. They looked like boxes because they had no wheels. All the men who lived here and some of the women, too, worked in the same plant as Dad. The plant owned the trailers and rented them to the people with jobs there, because there were no houses to rent. Trailers made very comfortable homes.

Boys and girls dashed out of the trailers, and a crowd had collected by the time the Book Bus drove up to Central Walk. It was blue, and a real bus. It had no windows on the sides, only in front and back. On one side there was a picture of some books, and, in large letters, SOUTHLAND BOOK BUS.

A girl in her early twenties was driving it. She had short, yellow hair, and there was something boyish about her wide smile. Don had to admire the expert way she brought the big bus to a stop.

"Hi, Miss Jackie!" shouted the children.

"Her name's Miss Jackson," a girl said to Dorry, "but everybody calls her Miss Jackie." Then she explained that the Book Bus came every Saturday.

Within the next few minutes, Dorry and the girl, whose name was Andrea, were friends. Andrea was amazed to learn that Dorry and Don were twins, because Don had dark, curly hair, Dorry straight, blond hair.

[4]

"I thought twins always looked alike," she said.

Miss Jackie opened the front door. Inside, the bus was like a house. The walls were lined with books clear up to the ceiling. The roof was made of glass to let in the daylight.

The children went in, a few at a time. Those who were outside formed a line to wait their turn. Everyone wore blue jeans—the girls as well as the boys.

Behind Don were several boys his age. One boy, called Ralph, who had a crew-cut and freckles, seemed to be the leader.

Suddenly, Ralph's voice grew loud. "I'm only going to let certain people use our clubhouse."

"Clubhouse!" hooted Andrea. "Ralph's sounding off about *that* again! How do you boys think you're going to get a clubhouse here in Trailer City?"

Ralph scowled. "We will. Someday. You'll see."

"Sure. You'll see!" The other boys took up the cry. "We've just *got* to have a place of our own."

One said, "I get sick of being chased all the time."

Another said, "No television in this part of South Carolina. No movies in Trailer City. What do they expect us to do?"

"Well, we've got the Book Bus," one girl replied.

"What fun is reading?" grumbled Ralph.

Don understood how he felt. Books weren't fun. The only ones he read were his school books.

"Why, reading is wonderful!" protested Dorry.

"Reading's O. K. for girls," Don admitted.

"Sure, for girls!" repeated Ralph. "But for boys, well, we've got to have real fun. Look, new guy," he addressed Don, "I bet you don't know anything about clubhouses!"

"Yes, I do," Don answered. "Back home in Ohio, another boy and I had one. A tree house. My Dad helped us build it out of a whopping big hogshead."

"Say, I bet that was slick!" said one of the other boys.

All the boys were looking at Don the way they had looked and listened to Ralph a moment before. Ralph did not seem to like this. He raised his voice again. "I don't believe it!" he told Don.

Dorry started to say that it was true. But just then the

line moved up, and Don and the others near him went into the Book Bus.

Dorry was right at home. She helped herself to some of the books, and sat down on one of the low benches. "So many books! I want to read them all."

Andrea asked Miss Jackie for a book about Texas, and another girl wanted one about Florida. "We're moving there," she said.

Miss Jackie knew where all the books were. She handed each girl a book. Then she announced, "You boys and girls who have no library cards must fill out these slips with your name and trailer number, and have your mother or father sign them." She gave a slip to Dorry and one to Don. "After you bring these back signed, you'll get a card, and then you may each take out two books every week."

Dorry looked ready to cry. "They have to be signed, *first?*"

Don said he wouldn't mind running home with the blanks for Mom to sign.

He was a good runner, and reached the trailer in no time

at all. He would have been there sooner, except he almost went to the wrong trailer! Theirs was on the last street in Trailer City, and was numbered O-15. The "O" was the name of the street. The streets began at "A" and went on to "O." Fifteen was the number of the trailer.

Soon Don was back at the Book Bus with the signed slips.

My, there were a lot of books! He counted across the bookcase and then up, and then multiplied the two numbers. Nearly one hundred books in that case alone. There

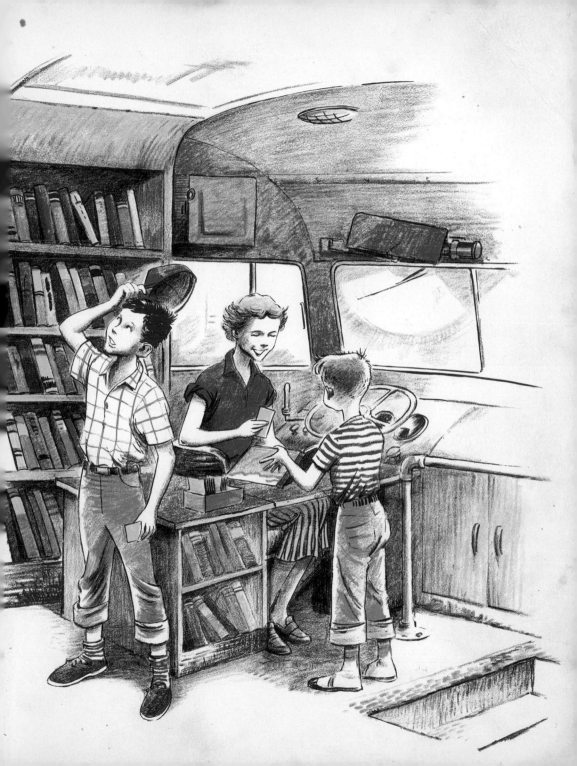

were eight such bookcases, not counting the shelves under the benches where the large books were, for the youngest readers.

"Why, there are nearly a thousand books here!"

Miss Jackie smiled as she took the slips. "Eight hundred. Surely you can find one you like."

Don hadn't planned to take out a book, but Miss Jackie seemed to expect him to use his new card. He looked around. A book with the title *How to Make Things* caught his eye. He skimmed through it, then put it back. What good was a book like that when you lived in a trailer twenty-eight feet long? There was no room to make anything.

A little later, Don noticed that Ralph had the same book open to the chapter, "How to Build a Clubhouse." Don felt he might have liked Ralph if only he had believed what Don told him about his tree house.

"I'm not going to take out any books," he told Dorry.

"Then take two on your card for me. I can read four books fast."

That was true. Dorry was good at reading. She liked it.

She selected two more books and handed them to Don. Then they joined the line waiting to have Miss Jackie stamp their books with the due date. Dorry and Andrea left with their books.

Suddenly, Ralph was there breathing down Don's neck.

Behind him were several other boys. They were the last of the Book Bus visitors.

"You taking out a book called *The Secret Garden?* Ya, where's your hair ribbon, Pretty Boy?" Ralph rumpled Don's hair. Then he snatched the book and tossed it high.

"Careful, boys! The skylight!" Miss Jackie hurried over to make peace.

Ralph twisted his leg around Don's and made him topple over to the floor. Don jumped up and struck out at Ralph, even though Ralph was so big.

Miss Jackie was beside them in an instant. Her presence had a quieting effect on both boys.

"We can't have anything like this on the Book Bus," she announced calmly. "Ralph, I believe you started everything. Better get your books stamped right away and go on home now. It's almost closing time, you know."

Ralph did not want to go home, but he knew Miss Jackie meant what she said. He took as much time as possible selecting his books, but finally he and the other boys filed out the door with their books under their arms.

Once outside the Book Bus, Ralph let out a loud whistle. "I'll see you later, Pretty Boy!" he shrilled.

Don and Miss Jackie were alone in the Book Bus. Don did not feel very comfortable about leaving just then. But if it was nearly closing time—

Miss Jackie seemed to understand perfectly. "Would you like to stay and help me tidy up a bit?" she asked.

Don did not want to tangle with Ralph again. He took the broom which Miss Jackie offered and began to sweep the floor.

Next, Don picked up some books the other children had left on the desk. When he started to put them on the nearest shelf, Miss Jackie came over and explained that each book has its own place in a library.

"A place where it belongs," she said. "See those numbers?" She held the book so he could see J-090 on the back. "The 'J' means juvenile—that is, children's—and the number shows its classification, or subject. Each book has a number."

"Like the trailers," Don said. "I guess that book's glad to

get home." He picked up another. It was soiled and sticky. "Kids ought to wash their hands before they pick up a book."

Miss Jackie grinned. "You'd make a good page."

"A page? Like in a book?"

"No. Our helpers are called pages." She studied him for a moment, then asked, "Did Ralph hurt you?"

"No, ma'am." Don forgot how his leg had ached when Ralph twisted it.

"Ralph's not really a bad boy." Miss Jackie seemed to be talking to herself. "It's just that there's nothing for boys his age to do here in Trailer City."

Don remembered one of the neighbors talking to Mom that very morning, saying almost the same thing. The mothers were worried about the "in-between-age" children. The younger ones had a playground and the older boys had a ball field. When Don tried to get into a ball game earlier that morning, the bigger boys had chased him off the field.

"I wish you in-betweeners had that clubhouse Ralph's

always talking about," Miss Jackie went on. "Then he could work off his high spirits there, instead of here. Roughhousing doesn't do this old bus a bit of good."

It was an old bus. Don could see that. Couldn't the library folks afford a new one, he wondered.

Miss Jackie read his thoughts. "We may get a new one soon. Not that it will mean anything to Trailer City."

Don looked puzzled. "You mean the Book Bus may stop coming here?"

Miss Jackie nodded. "The trouble is, the Trailer City folks don't seem to appreciate our services. We've been coming here on a trial basis. Mr. Riggs, head man on our library board, agreed to that. But the trial period will be over next month, around Thanksgiving." She sighed. "Well, thanks for helping me."

When Don left the Book Bus, he felt happier than he had been all day. He enjoyed helping Miss Jackie.

He walked back to the trailer and found that Dorry had already started reading the books. While waiting for dinner, Don wished he had that book called *How to Make*

Things. He wished, too, that Trailer City had a clubhouse.

That evening when Don was in his pajamas and ready to jump into his bunk, he heard sniffles from the studio couch in the living room where Dorry was to sleep. "What's the matter?" he asked. "You crying?"

She looked up from her book. "Guess so. It's this book. It's such a sad book. I just love sad books!"

Girls are dumb, Don thought; but at the same time he realized how terrible Dorry would feel if the Book Bus stopped coming to Trailer City.

Ralph and the other boys heard about Don helping Miss Jackie. All week they yelled, "Hi, Library Page! Page Boy! Here, Boy!" as though they were calling a dog. Don stayed out of their way.

On Saturday the Book Bus came again. Don went just to see what was going on, and Miss Jackie said, "Don, I'm glad you're here. I need you."

Don really worked. He put books back in their right places. He helped the children find the books they wanted.

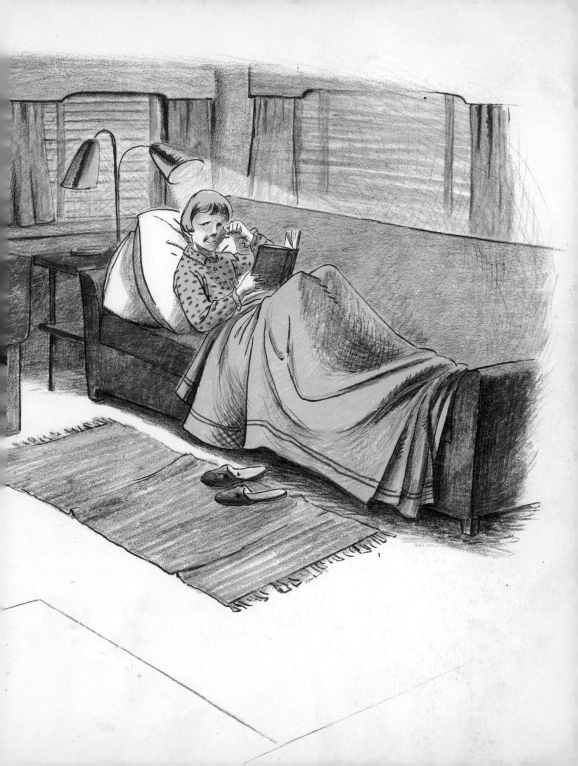

One boy asked for a book on raising guppies; another boy wanted a book on how to train a dog.

One little boy thrust a book at Don. "Read to me," he shouted.

So Don read until the youngster said, "O. K., I want that one."

After the children left, Don swept the floor and Miss Jackie tidied up the Book Bus. She talked about books while she worked. She told him about the title page, which showed who wrote the story, who drew the pictures, and who published the book. She showed him a Table of Contents, which listed the titles of the chapters and the number of the page on which each chapter began. Miss Jackie had a way of making books seem interesting.

Sunday it rained. There was nothing to do. Don picked up one of Dorry's books and was surprised to see that its title was *The Adventures of Tom Sawyer*. A boy's book?

He began to read. The book started out all right, with someone calling "Tom!" The words in the book weren't

hard; and before he knew it, Don was reading on, page after page. My, the boys in this book were real! They had fights, just the way he and Ralph had, but they were friends too.

The first thing he knew, Dad was shaking his arm. "Don! It's time for supper."

He must have read all afternoon! "Why, you know, Dad, when you read a book like this, it's just as if you were really there!"

"I know. That's a good book. Both Mom and I have read it."

That gave Don a warm, grown-up feeling inside.

He saw that Dorry had set the table and was now putting out peanut butter, jelly, cheese, cold cuts, and rye bread. Sunday supper was always sandwiches.

"That sure is a good book," he said as he made his favorite sandwich of peanut butter and catsup. "When I finish it, I may read it again."

Dorry nodded. "That's what's nice about reading. And you can take books around with you, too."

"You know sumpin'?" Don mumbled with his mouth full. "Reading's fun!"

"Haven't I been telling you?"

Don was beginning to understand now how Dorry could curl up and be happy with a book. Why, he need never be lonely as long as there were stories to read.

He thought of the books that lined the Book Bus, and how he had wondered what was inside all of them. Then he remembered—the bus might not be coming to Trailer City much longer! He would have to read fast while he had the chance.

When Saturday came again, there was the Book Bus and he selected two books that looked good. But Dorry blocked his way to the checking desk. Her blue eyes blazed. "Donald Tracy, that's not fair! Last week you said I could take books on your card."

"That was last week." Don's voice rose. "This week I've changed my mind." He couldn't fight Dorry, though his fist was clenched. "Dorothy Tracy, remember, I'm older than you are!"

So he was. Fifteen minutes older. Usually he was able to squelch her with this, but not now.

Miss Jackie hurried over and, quick as a sneeze, she had four books that both of them liked. Two of them were *Really True* books. Miss Jackie called such books "nonfiction," and she called storybooks "fiction."

As the days went by, Don read and read. It was as though he couldn't get enough of reading. It was like the time he had been sick. When he got better, he couldn't seem to get enough to eat.

Mom and Dad took out library cards, too.

The Tracy family began reading aloud in the evening. To his surprise, Don found he enjoyed this. "But," he complained to Dad, "there's still nothing for us boys to *do*."

"Like what?" asked Dad.

"Like—well, if we had a clubhouse of our own we'd find plenty to do." He told Dad about a book he had read in which some boys and girls fixed over an old, unused cottage. They had painted it inside and out, and the girls

had tinted muslin for curtains. "But here in Trailer City . . ." He paused.

Dad understood. "When I was a boy, we made a fine house out of a piano box. But when you live in a trailer, no one has a piano!"

"But, Dad, if we could get some lumber, and if the renting agent would let us have one of the empty spaces, maybe—"

"Maybe," was all Dad would say. But Don knew his father wanted them to have a clubhouse, too.

Ralph happened to be in the Book Bus one day when Don handed the *How to Make Things* book to Miss Jackie. He wanted to have it stamped on his library card.

"Hey, wise guy!" Ralph glared at him. "You can't have that book. Everybody knows I wanted it."

"Well, I didn't know," Don told him.

Ralph looked ready to fight, but Miss Jackie said, "Don got here first." She stamped the book and handed it to him.

Dad was too busy to talk about plans for a clubhouse. Don had to dream of it by himself. He wondered if Ralph got tired of dreaming and waiting, too? He heard that Ralph was spending his after-school hours in town with a few of the older boys who play the juke boxes and pinball machines. "Just juking around," was the way Ralph put it. "Maybe we'll break a window or two—anything for some excitement."

The following Friday was Armistice Day. No school!

After lunch, Dorry reminded Don, "The girls are coming to our trailer. Mom's helping us start a Girl Scout troop."

Don was glad when Mom suggested he take the bus to town to a movie.

When he reached the highway, he decided to hike to town, and he had not gone far when a big, blue bus drew up and stopped.

"Hi!" Miss Jackie greeted him. "Want a ride? Want to go with me on my stops this afternoon?"

"I'd like it!" Don hopped up the steps of the Book Bus. Miss Jackie flipped the lever that closed the door after

[35]

him, and motioned to a piece of paper stuck under the windshield wiper. "Those are the stops we'll make."

Don read the list.

"No school stops today," Miss Jackie told him, as he took his place on the seat next to her. "They're fun. Grade by grade, the children in country schools come down to the Book Bus. My trip really starts in town, at the big library, where I pick the books for the day's stops."

The first stop was a housing development—streets and streets of small houses. There were trees, too.

The folks who lived here were glad to see Miss Jackie. The mothers swarmed into the Book Bus. One woman came in a wheel chair. Miss Jackie sent Don out with an armful of books so the woman could pick what she wanted.

Next, they headed for the country. They passed miles of peach orchards. The trees were bare and brown. Soon, they pulled up at a country store. A poster announcing the Book Bus schedule was displayed in the window. A crowd had gathered to wait. They were carrying books, and they shouted, "Here she comes!" when Miss Jackie drove up.

Some of the women had babies in their arms, and youngsters tugging at their skirts. Miss Jackie had lollipops for the children.

Men came, too, carrying books wrapped up in newspapers because their hands were soiled from working in the barns.

A boy Don's age wanted a book on baseball. Don showed him where to find it, and the two got acquainted.

As they started off again, Miss Jackie remarked, "Well, you and George got along fine. And so could you and Ralph, if he weren't afraid the other Trailer City boys might like you better than they do him."

That was a new idea to Don.

"You and Ralph would make a good team," she added.

Going home, Miss Jackie began to drive fast. The sky had darkened. It looked as though a storm were coming.

Miss Jackie chatted all the way home, and she drove Don almost to Trailer City, along the muddy road just beyond "O" street.

The engine was knocking. It sounded like ping-pong balls in a fast game. "This old bus needs to be completely rebuilt," Miss Jackie said.

As she spoke, the engine coughed and went dead.

"Sounds bad." Miss Jackie got out of the bus, looked under the hood at the engine, then said, "I'll have to get a mechanic. I'll phone for one. You stay here and take care of the books."

Don felt important as he moved the lever to close the door. Then he picked out several books and settled himself in the driver's seat.

The clock on the dash panel said four o'clock, but it was getting dark. Still, Don did not turn on the lights.

The minutes passed slowly.

The wind howled around the Book Bus. What if the mechanic did not come for a long time? What if he had to stay here all night?

Someone was running through the gloom outside, running toward the Book Bus. It was Ralph. "What's the big idea of the Book Bus coming today? And stopping *here?*" he demanded when he was close enough to recognize Don.

Don spoke through the crack in the closed door. "This isn't a regular Book Bus day."

"I know that," snapped Ralph. "But I want a book. I've got my card in my pocket."

"I'm sorry," began Don slowly. He did not want to anger Ralph. "But Miss Jackie has all her stamps put away. Besides, I can't let you take out a book."

Ralph's face looked mean. "You don't need to *let* me take out a book. I'll come in and take it myself."

"No, you won't," Don answered.

"Open up this door, Tracy!" ordered Ralph.

Don did not move.

A shower of pebbles splashed at the sides of the Book Bus, some of them hitting the cab window beside Don. He jumped up. A thumping sound made him stand still. Pieces of glass rained down from the roof. Ralph had broken the skylight with a rock.

"That does it. I'll fix him." Don jerked the door open, tumbled down the steps, and ran after the other boy. He caught up with him before Ralph reached the gate of the tall, steel wire fence.

"All right, put 'em up." He backed Ralph against the fence.

"Don't want to," Ralph mumbled.

"Well, we're going to fight this out, right now," Don warned him, and squared off. "Ready?"

Ralph was a good fighter and heavier than Don; but Don was faster, better at dodging blows. Soon Ralph was on the ground, and Don was sitting on his chest. He had to watch out for Ralph's feet and his heavy boots.

"Give up? Had enough?" Don panted.

"Nuff!" Ralph's voice was hoarse.

Don let him up then, and held out his hand. "Shake?"

Ralph ignored Don's outstretched hand. He brushed past and hurried through the gate toward Trailer City. As he ran, he held both hands to his face. Was he crying? Boys of his age didn't cry!

Don shrugged, then plodded through the mud back to the Book Bus. He had beaten Ralph. He should feel happy, but he didn't.

Anyway, there was no time for him to think. He had to clean up that broken glass. He got out the broom and dustpan and set to work.

The whole skylight was broken. Don looked through

at the dark clouds. It was going to rain—and soon. What should he do? He had nothing to put over the great open place, and no ladder to climb up to the roof of the bus anyway. He might borrow a ladder and a poncho or something from one of the nearby trailers. But, even so, how could he make any covering stay in place up there? You could not put nails in a steel roof; and nothing would stay on without nailing, not in this howling wind.

If, or rather when, the rain started, the books on the shelves would get wet. He knew the library bindings on the books were tough, but the books themselves were not waterproof.

He began moving some of the books from the shelves and piling them up near the driver's seat, out of range of the broken skylight.

As he worked, he peered out of the window, watching. If anyone went by within hailing distance, he would call for help. But no one did. Trailer City appeared to be completely deserted.

Don thought he felt a drop of rain through the skylight.

He had to do something! He couldn't wait for Miss Jackie and the mechanic to get back. The rain would soon be pouring through the skylight.

Don remembered a story he had read about a boys' school, and how they saved books in a fire by forming a brigade and passing the books from one boy to another and out to safety.

Don knew he could not get any Trailer City boys to help him. The older boys were away at the Armistice Day ceremonies. And Ralph's gang certainly wouldn't help him *now*.

But—what about those girls who were meeting in O-15 right this moment?

Don darted through the gloom and reached O-15 in double-quick time.

Giggles floated out as he opened the door. He saw the girls sitting on the studio couch and on the floor, grouped around Mom, who was reading from the Girl Scout handbook.

Dorry tried to hold the door shut. "Boys not allowed!

You promised!" She appealed to Mom. "Mom, make him stay out, please."

But Mom seemed to know this was an emergency. She let Don in, and he told them about the Book Bus.

"Oh, we'll help you, Don! It will be our good deed for today."

Mom stopped the girls from running out of the trailer. "No matter how willing you are, you can't carry eight hundred books."

Don was looking out through the window. He saw several Trailer City mothers pushing canvas strollers, scurrying home ahead of the coming storm.

"Mom! Strollers would hold a lot of books. There are dozens of strollers we could borrow." Don's words tumbled out.

"H-m-m, a good idea," Mom agreed. "And we'll have to take some things to cover the books and the card catalogue files."

Quickly she told the girls where they could borrow strollers. Most of the girls had brought their rain slickers

with them, and they put them on. Mom fixed up the others with the family ponchos and rain coats.

Mom hurried back to the Book Bus with Don. They took quilts, and rubber sheets, and plastic tablecloths with them.

They began taking books from the shelves, to have them ready when the girls came.

As the girls came up to the door of the Book Bus with the borrowed strollers, Mom and Don began to load them.

Eight hundred books. Twenty girls. That came to about forty books for each load. Some strollers held less, some more. Many of the strollers had canvas covers that could be snapped closed over the books.

"Don's captain of the baby-buggy brigade," one girl said.

The others began chanting, "Captain Don, Captain Don."

"Forty, forty-one, forty-two," counted Mom. "That's enough. Put them on the floor of the bedroom in our trailer, girls."

One load apiece would be enough, Mom said. But when she sent the last girl off, there were still some books around.

"I'll take care of these." Mom shoved as many as she could under the driver's seat. She told Don to tuck an old leather coat around the card files. In their steel boxes, the records would be safe.

Just as they were taking a final look around the bus, Miss Jackie appeared in the doorway.

"I simply can't get a mechanic anywhere." She stopped, her eyes enormous. "Why, what on earth happened?"

They explained to Miss Jackson. Then they made a run for O-15. They reached it just as the storm broke.

The morning sun slanted in and woke Don. He turned over on his elbow, and all he could see was books.

Was he sleeping in the Book Bus? Then he remembered all that had happened the day before.

Where had Mom and Dad slept? Oh yes, now he remembered, they had taken the studio coach, and Dorry spent the night at Andrea's. Dorry probably had not yet returned. Don looked at the clock and guessed that Dad was at work and Mom was at the store.

He jumped into his jeans, and was pulling on his T-shirt, when he heard a sound outside. Expecting to see Dorry, Don hardly glanced toward the door when it opened.

Instead, it was Ralph.

"Ma said I had to come," he began hesitantly. "She says you're a hero! Saw your Mom at the store, and she said I'd find you here."

Don waited for him to go on.

"Your Mom said you were tired from yesterday and she let you sleep. She had a message to telephone Miss Jackie at the library."

At that, Don crossed to the rear window of the trailer. He knelt on the studio coach and peered out. The Book Bus looked better, now that the mud and dust had been washed from it by the rain. But what good was that? The bus might not be coming to Trailer City any more.

"I didn't mean to break the skylight on the Book Bus," Ralph went on. "I forgot the roof was glass. And say, you're a good fighter, Tracy."

"But, Ralph, you wouldn't even shake hands!"

"Couldn't. My nose was bleeding something fierce." He stuck out his hand now and Don took it.

Why, Ralph was nice. They could be friends! Maybe they could work together for a clubhouse for Trailer City.

Just at that moment, Dorry burst into the trailer. She stood, mouth open. Her eyes popped. "You two— friends?"

"Sure," Don said.

"But he's been so mean to you, Don. You know you have, Ralph!"

Ralph mumbled something, but Dorry didn't listen.

[60]

"Oh, you made me forget the wonderful, wonderful news! Miss Jackie was so happy that we found a way to save the books. She told Mom that proved Trailer City folks appreciate reading. The library board's going to get a *new* Book Bus and Trailer City will be a regular stop." She paused, out of breath.

The two boys stared at each other. Both started to speak.

"What's going to happen to the old bus?" asked Don.

"What about the old bus?" asked Ralph.

Then they snickered because each had said the same thing.

Don had a sudden idea. "Say! Maybe—maybe—we could—" He was so excited, he couldn't get the words out.

Ralph was trying to say something, too. "Do you suppose we could—?"

"—have it for our clubhouse?" shouted both boys.

"You mean," asked Dorry, "a clubhouse for the in-betweeners?"

"Sure!" Ralph bobbed his head. "We can fix it up."

"Like those kids in that book," added Don.

"Will you let the girls use it?" asked Dorry.

"Girls' Day once a week," Ralph decided.

Dorry rushed out of the trailer to tell Andrea.

The boys hardly knew what to do first. When Mom came in, she listened to their plan, and said they should telephone Miss Jackie.

They hurried to the telephone at the store. They were glad it was Saturday and they had time to work on this important project.

Miss Jackie liked their idea. "The man to see is Mr. Riggs. He will be here at the library this afternoon," she told them. "I'll make an appointment for you to see him at three o'clock."

How could they ever wait till then?

Right after lunch both boys got dressed in their Sunday best.

On their way to the highway for the bus to town, they stopped to look the Book Bus over. It would be the swellest clubhouse any guys ever had, they told each other. All the way in to town, they talked about the old bus.

It would be just the right size. They could have quiet games at one end. Maybe target games with rubber darts at the other. And books? Of course!

They would paint it a plain color and cover the walls with their autographs. The girls would take care of curtains for the windows. Of course, their mothers would help. Maybe their fathers, too.

They just *had* to get the old bus for a clubhouse!

The town library was in a building that had once been a

big white house. The girl at the desk in the hall was expecting them. She sent them up the wide stairway to Mr. Riggs's office.

Mr. Riggs was a kindly man, with white hair and a smiling face. Don liked him right away.

"Miss Jackson tells me you boys want to use the old Book Bus for a clubhouse for Trailer City," he said.

"Yes, sir!" they replied.

"Well, I've just been talking with the renting agent at Trailer City, and—" His blue eyes sparkled. "Our library board will rent a space out there in Trailer City, and the Book Bus will be set up on it. It will be your clubhouse. The library board will act as sponsors, with the parents' help. Yes, boys, you'll have your clubhouse."

"Oh, thank you, sir!" said Ralph.

"Thank you very much, Mr. Riggs," added Don, though he could hardly believe the good news.

"We'll work out details later on. I just wanted you to know the news." Mr. Riggs was dismissing them, so the boys said good-bye and went out.

Going down the steps, Ralph turned to grin at Don. And Don grinned back. "A clubhouse!" Ralph sounded as though he couldn't believe it, either. "Golly, we'll be busy fixing it up!"

"*And*—I know just the book to help us," said Don.

THE TEXT *of this book has been set on the Monotype in a type face named Bembo.*

COMPOSED *by Westcott & Thomson, Inc., Philadelphia.*

PRINTED *by Reehl Litho Company, Inc., New York.*

BOUND *by H. Wolff, New York.*

TYPOGRAPHY *by Charles Farrell.*